Memory Man
& Other Poems

Memory Man
& Other Poems

Ian Watson

LEAKY BOOT PRESS

Memory Man & Other Poems
by Ian Watson

First published in 2014 by
Leaky Boot Press
http://www.leakyboot.com

ISBN: 978-1-909849-11-2

CONTENTS

THREE TOKYO POEMS
FROM AROUND 1970

POEMS & LYRICS FROM
NOVELS AND STORIES

MANA POEMS

BALLADS, SONGS AND TANGO

COLLABORATIONS WITH MIKE ALLEN

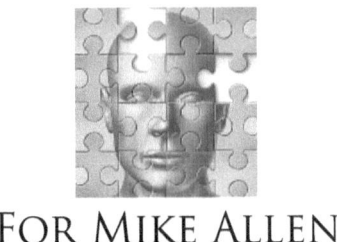

FOR MIKE ALLEN

ME AND THE MUSE

I suppose I started writing scraps of poetry when I was 14 or so; I remember something about orchids on a canoe in the Amazon—exotic, topographical, brooding, far removed from the North-East of England of my upbringing. I had been much taken by the woodcut illustrations in Henry Bates' *The Naturalist on the River Amazons*. In 1959—when I was 16 and had left school because I'd already passed all the exams; I don't *remember* being a swot—I visited my aunt in London 250 miles away by bus (about 12 hours in those days before motorways) and bought a copy of Lawrence Durrell's *Selected Poems* (1956), yellow cloth back, yellow dust cover. I sought for short lyrical topographical poetry set in non-English locations, and this book pretty much fitted the bill. I still remember "The Pleiades":"The Pleiades are sinking cool as paint/While Earth's huge camber follows out/Turning in sleep, the oceanic curve." I aimed for Durrell because his naturalist brother Gerald's *My Family and Other Animals*, about life and wildlife on Corfu, was a joy of my childhood, and one day I wondered whether 'Larry' ever became a writer. Yes, he did—and his *Justine* (not de Sade's) was in my local library to puzzle me somewhat at my tender age.

The other poetry hardback I bought on that visit to London was *Talking Bronco* by Roy Campbell because there was an animal in the title and Campbell was South African, so I thought there ought to be poems about elephants and giraffes, and indeed I believe there was one about giraffes called "Dreaming Spires". Campbell's satire and his tough-guy attitudes, which led him to support Franco (though he never actually fought, and was anti-Nazi as well as fluent in Zulu, lampooning racism)—these largely passed me by, though his translation of St John of the Cross's "Upon a gloomy night, with all my cares to loving ardours flushed ..." affected me, erotically rather than spiritually; Borges surmised that Campbell's version might be better than the Spanish original. Talking of spirits, on that visit to my aunt I first encountered punch, at a party in an American diplomat's flat, and became so sick that 50 years later I still can't stand the taste or smell of gin—aversion therapy works.

So I was fairly confused in my poetical influences and motivations. Robert Graves appealed to me, led to his poetry by *I, Claudius* and *Claudius the God*. Also I'd bought in a second-hand shop in a Newcastle market an anthology of so-called 'Modern' American Poetry where the star turns for me were Emily Dickinson and Nicholas Vachel Lindsay's "The Congo" with its pounding rhythms. "Blackback bucks in a wine-barrel room/ Barrel-house kings with feet unstable/Sagged and reeled and pounded on the table/Pounded on a table with the handle of a broom/Boomlay-boomlay-boomlay-boom..." (All quotations here are from memory and unverified, so they may be a bit inaccurate.) Rhythm is something I value in poetry. Rhymes can occur or half-occur as they please, but a poem without rhythm is just plain prose chopped up to look like a poem. The downside of rhythm is the potential for doggerel.

A good thing about poems for me as a lad was their comparative shortness—I could foresee the proverbial slim volume of verse.

Since I read English Literature at Oxford, I perforce soaked up a fair amount more poetry; W. B. Yeats intoxicated me. Postgraduately, I absorbed some Baudelaire and Rimbaud.

When I was living in East Africa, the poets of Negritude (francophone colonial black pride with, to me, a surreal stripe) such as Léopold Sédar Senghor, some time President of Senegal, had quite an effect. Subsequently, there was Wallace Stevens: "A man bent over his guitar/A shearsman of sorts, the day was green..."

In short, an eclectic—or chaotic—set of influences.

In the 70s I ventured to teach to the Fashion Students of Birmingham Art School a highly unsystematic course on modern world poetry, such writers as Hungarians Sándor Weöres and Ferenc Juhász, and Germans Hans Magnus Enzensberger (who provided the epigraph for my *Jonah Kit*, and was very amiable in doing so, as was his translator Michael Hamburger) and Günther Grass.

I really began writing (and parodying) poetry in earnest if some poetry was needed for my novels; it seemed unreasonable to feature a poet as a character in fiction unless I also provided at least a sample of the poet's work. Thus in *Deathhunter* the fictional poet Norman Harper, whom I quickly assassinate, delivers bittersweet banalities in the greetings card style of Robert Frost:

The embryo bird must partly die
If its wings are to emerge, to fly.
The caterpillar dies, as well,
To become the butterfly, so swell...

and so on for quite a while (included later in this collection).

This bad bard also butchered a masterly sonnet by Friedrich Hölderlin, "To the Fates", into a saccharine parody (also included). My evoking Hölderlin doesn't actually mean that I read all that much by him, even though I find I can quote the first verse of "To the Fates" in German. I was a bit like a hummingbird as regards poetry, hovering to suck some nectar before flicking onward to a different flower. The poet whose works I read most of is undoubtedly Chaucer, namely the complete *Canterbury Tales* in Middle English, because I had to—well, I don't suppose I actually *had* to read the whole caboodle; but this stood me in good stead near the start of my authorly career when I was interviewed on the BBC by Robert Robinson for *Today*, the BBC's flagship morning news show compèred by RR, and we enthusiastically bonded by quoting the General Prologue at each other in Middle English.

In my 1988 novel *Whores of Babylon* I wanted two of my

characters to visit a performance of Euripides's *Andromeda*, Euripides being the most modernist of the great Greek tragedians. Unfortunately this play by him got lost, so I was obliged to invent a long soliloquy from it, in the style of a 19th Century translator. Andromeda was chained to an offshore rock by her Dad as a sacrifice to a ravaging sea monster, either in Ethiopia or at Jaffa in Israel. Subsequently I was invited to Israel, and the event kicked off in Jaffa with me declaiming my soliloquy to the night-dark sea followed by an Israeli actress declaiming my soliloquy in Hebrew. Or vice versa.

Things looked up as regards more poetical poetry in the 1990s, with my Finnish-inspired science fantasy magnum opus epic, *The Books of Mana* (consisting of *Lucky's Harvest* and *The Fallen Moon*), because these included a good poet, name of Eyeno, who only had one eye—her name also being an allusion to the Finnish poet Eino Leino, whose statue has (or had) its back to the superloo on the way to Helsinki harbour, and whose *Whitsongs*—ballad-like symbolist legend-capsules in the vein of the *Kalevala*—kicked off my very long (for me) double-novel about the power of language to shape reality; consequently the words ought to be as evocative as I could make them. "Otherwhys" and "Wintermute" are poems of mine which first appeared in magazines. In *The Books of Mana* I assigned these two poems to Eyeno. Thus both poems appear here in the main section rather than in the "Mana" section, although nowadays I regard my character Eyeno as the author. Other Yeatsian-flavoured Finnish-tango-mood ballads from the novel are, for instance, this, out of the mouth of a dwarf brass robot:

Sky-sickle shines upon the sea
Silver combs in your hair
You're as far away from me
Without a care, without a care...

For short narrative passages in verse I deliberately followed the *tumti-tumti* Longfellow *Hiawatha* rhythm of the original translation of the *Kalevala* (which is soporific pants, compared with Keith Bosley's far more flexibly muscular and lyrical version, though fun for a while). All of the Mana poetry which can stand independently is in this collection.

Indeed I wrote the *Books of Mana* in a kind of poetic afflatus that lasted for two years, ramping up my prose to match. Then in the late 90s I stepped up poetry production because for several years my wife Judy was heading downhill and time was increasingly taken up by wheelchair, oxygen cylinders, cooking to a high standard, and lots of other demands upon a carer. Poetry was a way I could keep on writing even if my available time increasingly (or decreasingly) shrank; for how can a writer not write? For a while poetry was the only light in a dark tunnel. If I couldn´t manage a short story, at least I could manage a poem, revised many times. And I realised that a flourishing community of science fiction poets existed, many belonging to the admirable Science Fiction Poetry Association, founded by Suzette Haden Elgin, whose novel *Native Tongue* is a high point of linguistics in science fiction. And American SF poet and ace reporter Mike Allen of *Mythic Delirium* became my email friend, resulting in several poetical collaborations, as well as in publication of my first poetry chapbook, *The Lexicographer's Love Song*, in 2001, edited and designed by himself and his wife Anita, with a lovely cover and internal illustrations by Tim Mullins.

A while later, Mike and Anita visited me in England, and one day I drove them to the gorgeous gardens of Hidcote Manor, since Anita and I are very keen on plants. There, Mike conceived his dark and twisted poem 'The Night Gardeners' ('shapes move beneath the shroud of night; the night gardeners crawl from the soil/to tend blooms in the hours of unlight...'), and on the same day our merry or mentally deranged collaboration 'Propitiating Cthulhu' was spawned.

And the poetical impetus has carried on....

ABDUCTEE

When the amorphous Greys,
Slippery oversize foetuses
With eyes as big as saucers,
Rapture and rape you
From your bed of dreams
Into their bright and mutable
Vehicle which defies our ken,
You retain a sceptical edge.

You don't disbelieve in
The possibility of alien visitors
But you know the illusory nature
Of human witness: such a history
Of visions, apparitions, angels,
Fairies, innumerable miracles
Which are all as unprovable
As the voices a madman hears,
The hallucinations he sees.

Do you experience abduction,
Melissa? Oh yes, undoubtedly.
Can this truly be happening? No.
Inside us all may exist many minds,
Semi-intelligent and semi-sovereign,
This whole ensemble of sub-systems
Sustaining the person, me.
Can these Greys perhaps be

Your very own sub-sets
Out for a night on the tiles?

Pesky sleek elusive dwarfs:
No way are those higher entities.
Their conduct, on the contrary,
Is childish, impish, and inane.
They must be lower mentalities
From the recesses of your brain.
But wait, since they have free rein
How can you still be *yourself*?

The process of mind is opaque
To introspection, not so?
Maybe not tonight, when
Your sub-sets frolic around you
Like the apprentice sorcerer's broom!
Ah, they are only cerebral systems,
Various shuttles in the loom!
What of your sovereign soul, Melissa?
Of your soul, what shall we presume?

What if your consciousness is not
A product of sub-sets at all?
What if it stems from a psyche
Common to all humankind,
Awareness shared mutually,
Melissa, by you and by me?
What if the author and source
Of your self and your thoughts
Is not yourself, after all,
But is the whole of humanity?

Your mind is a vehicle for thoughts
Yet you don't own the thoughts, as such,
Which channel themselves through you.
A psychosphere in space and time

Emits the beam that lights the mind,
Common thoughts, common words
Forging your sense of identity.

Mask-faced Greys are marionettes
Pulling their own strings tonight.
But you too are a mask, Melissa,
One of billions of guises worn
By Generalissimo Consciousness.
Her words and thoughts are strings
Jerking the dance of your days
And of all of her private soldiers
In the great identity parade.

This is your vision, Melissa,
A glimpse of an overview:
Abducted by yourself, you find
There never was a self to lose.

Andromeda

ANDROMEDA (*in chains*):

Like the real Helen who never sailed to Troy
So that men and ships followed a ghost
And Priam's son loved a ghost in bed,
A hallucination sent by gods to craze men,
Or by one goddess to save that selfsame Helen
From Paris's lust and from the blood debt
Of all the foolish heroes, and the ruin
Of great Troy for ever…
I am sacrificed for a phantom too,
The phantom of my father's pride,
Which irked an even more potent phantom,
Poseidon, figment of a sick imagination,
My sire's. But my death will be real
If the sea-dragon that ravages these shores
Is real; if it is not a guise for pirates
Who plunder, and can be bought off
With a chained virgin's blood
—Of pierced maidenhead!
Who could rescue me from this cruel rock
Unless he be a pirate too, of another stripe?
For what are heroes but pirates by another name
Who wage war on fate (or fatal circumstance)
And pluck from time the mantle of distinction,
Stealing from the gods the flame of immortality,
Robbing even the grave of its boon, oblivion?

Do not heroes seize the high ground of history
There to erect their image, their phallus
Of power to procreate not sons and daughters
But a name, the name of hero
Before which women must weep and pray?
And yet my soul yearns for a hero
—Just as, enchained, made vulnerable,
I yearn also for a pirate to pluck me
For then at least this will be over
When I will be a virgin prize no more.
And if the dragon-pirate and the hero
Could perhaps kill each other mutually
Leaving nearby for me to grasp
The hero's fallen blooded sword
And the pirate's sharp sea-serpent tooth
To saw my chains and shatter them
I could break free, escape, and be myself:
A priestess in some greensward temple
Close by a private fountain, where no
Intruder phantom god lurks and leers
To step out from the shade in shepherd's guise
Or rise from the depths disguised as a naiad
With budding breasts and tresses of gold,
Before revealing—himself. But I am torn
In my heart between the fear of ravage
—And the fear of rescue from ravage;
And the desire for both these fates
Which my father taught me long ago
And my mother too, conspiring with him
Every time she combed my hair out
And anointed me with fragrant oils.
I hear a growling on the shore, the clutch
Of claws—or are those boots and weapons
Of a man? I hear a sighing in the air,

A rushing fall, as if a horse could gallop
Through the clouds, its hooves beating
Blue-black bruises in their fleece
From which the raindrops fall
Which are the tears of heaven.
Who comes from the sea? Who comes
From the sky? A god? A man? A beast? A hero?
Or my own faint fears, shameful that they are,
The beating of my own heart in my breast,
The blood pounding in the bonds that hold me
Tight as a lover's embrace...

(**Author's Note**: Euripides, the most modernist of the great Greek tragedians, did write a play called *Andromeda*. Unfortunately the play was lost but I decided to invent part of it in translation for a novel of mine called *Whores of Babylon*. "The real Helen" refers to a legend probably originating with the Sicilian poet Stesichorus (c. 600 B.C) to the effect that the goddess Hera arranged for a simulacrum of Helen to elope to Troy with Paris, while the god Hermes carried the real Helen to Egypt where she lived under an alias till a ripe old age. Everyone was fooled, and thus the Trojan War was a farce.

Andromeda was chained to an offshore rock by her Dad as a sacrifice to a ravaging sea monster, either in Ethiopia or at Jaffa in Israel.)

Catalogue Note
by the Artist

Beyond violet there's ultraviolet; beyond red, infrared.
My eyes are wide; flowers glow long past dusk
While in the dark of night lovers shine hotly.
Reality has other dimensions hidden orthogonally
(as it's called) away from the customary four.
So I began to paint in subyellow and suprablue,
Colours perpendicular to the visible spectrum.
At a further right angle is my famous *J series*
In jed, jellow, jreen, jlue, jndigo, and jiolet.
Visitors to this gallery may perceive blank canvases
Although they will feel disconcerted
Since I depict my dreams and nightmares
Which can be sensed unseen as absent presences.
Some very challenging paintings seem invisible;
Obviously those ones cost the ultramost.

Cobwebs in Heaven

God's Wife wasn't like Eve—
although He created Eve in Her image.
She didn't just potter about in a garden
prior to a curse of childbirth and housework
and being ruled over by a man.

While He took a siesta on the Seventh Day
She was busy with Her own creations,
Which She rather hoped He'd admire,
the life of a million other worlds
—for She was quite a fast worker.

But He was furious and scorned those as toys
And threw her out of his house called Heaven.
Could it possibly be that He was *jealous*?
He'd only decorated one world; She'd equipped
Most of the rest of the universe.

Yet She wasn't too heart-broken, God's wife,
Satana, not when She thought about it,
falling through space towards her million Edens.

In His rage God forgot one little thing:
Who would keep His Heaven clean?
That's why He created angels as audience
to applaud Him while serving as feather dusters
to sweep away cobwebs with their wings.

Counterfactual Photos

Memories rewrite themselves; photos remind us
of what was actual: the green dress she was wearing
that Easter in Paris, sunglasses upon raven hair.

At least that's how it was till old photos
began to show what might have been true
in another life, alternative existences.

She isn't there at all; a thin blonde woman is,
black jeans, purple blouse, rings and necklaces,
and I'm in a lightweight cream suit I never owned.

After some weeks or months this photo too can change.
She's black as ebony and I have a neat beard
and the French café we're outside is a different one.

Photos in books don't alter, only personal ones
whether prints or data; history remains intact,
and our mutating memories of reality past.

"What was her name?" she asks me. How can I know?
She too has photos of herself with other men
whom obviously she never met. If she'd had the chance

and if I'd had the chance, who knows? So the photos
taunt and embarrass and, yes, *frustrate* us
with possibilities unfulfilled. Some couples split up

these days and search, years after those non-events,
although the youthful lover must be sixty by now.
Sometimes you see the kids you never had.

At first only photos from thirty-plus years ago
altered. But then: twenty-nine, twenty-eight,
the wave of alteration heading towards the present.

Governments are about to confiscate all private
cameras and camera phones; the Photo Police
will call on you; art schools are churning out illustrators.

The PP will install CCTVs in every home
unviewable by human eyes, scanned only by
impersonal reality-checking supercomputers.

Constant Eye, *C-AI*, like an all-seeing God,
will watch us while we live our lives, securing
a single future in the War Against Mutability.

DEATH BY DYSLEXIA

We tried to help daughter Amanda.
We really went out of our way.
As a rule she mixed "d" and "b"
So we'd say "Goob Bay," not "Good Day."
Dye-dye was bye-bye; *bog* was dog.
We would often call her Amanba,
Being extra helpful, right?
On the night when we went to the party
Best friend Deborah came to stay—
She only rarely laughed at Amanda.
Two peas in a pod with cocoa
—"Gosh Mummy, it's yummy"—
And Disney to watch from the bed.
Old enough to be on their ownsome
For a few hours, eh? As I hugged
Goobnight, did Deborah giggle a mite?
"Be sure to switch off when it's finished,
Amanba," I said. "Tick-tock, tick-tock:
"That's debby-dye-time, remember!"
"Debby-dye, Mummy," said she.
Alas, when we came back at midnight
Bed's dloob was all over the deb.
We tried to help darling Amanda.
We bib our dest, I'd say.
And now we send her mirror-letters
Since she has gone away.

ENTERTAINING A HOPE

My fingers make
Shadow rabbit ears
On the wall, I swing
A ribbon to and fro,
I pull funny faces
Until my hope laughs.
"Do you imagine
I was born yesterday?"

Shall I buy my hope
A lottery ticket?
Then she must linger
At least till Saturday.
Shall I write my hope
A poem so lovely
That she admires herself
As in a bathroom mirror
Till the words written
In steam fade away?

If you don't entertain a hope
What hope dare you have
That she'll stay?

Exprisonment

Hoops, glittering hoops drifting overhead:
last year they swooped on everyone—since when
Sean has a cage on his foot like mine on my right hand.

Behold Waist-Cage, and Head-Cage, and Knee-Cage
who walks with a clumsy swing to his stride.
A rod through my wrist fixes my hindrance,
a rod through Sean's ankle, his curse.
Such a piss-awful nuisance, our cages!
Painless to wear yet so very encumbering!
Dire pangs occur if there's sawing and surgery,
all in vain, since after a few days of agony
a hoop restores an identical impediment.

Hoops are bomb-proof. We can't see through 'em.
From beyond is an alien audience laughing at us?
Are we ripe for invasion yet? Or might we *deserve*
our impeds? Sean, who doted on dancing. Me, who…
 never you mind!

We go where we please and our cages accompany us.
So what's the opposite of imprisonment termed?

FONES

Flutterfones flock,
microprism wings iridescent
in the sunlight.

Fallen fones lie among
russet leaves, a few still
flapping though maimed.

Sentinels in trees, crows
will attack an airborne fone;
magpies will carry fones off.

New fones forever
unfurl and fly free
from the telecom farms.

People beckon; fones settle,
through our implants read
our identity—end call, fly away.

If you wish, they'll stay
and personalise to you.
Mine nestles folded

In my jacket breast pocket;
three months it's kept me
company, learning my ways.

Unfold, fone, fly to my ear,
droop a wing by my mouth.
I just have to think: dial *her*

And it knows, and obliges;
but instead of herself
Anna's persona answers

And although the persona
assures me of love I feel
such jealousy and alienation.

FOSSIL MAN

Mister Stone, Mister Stone, when you die
You'll neither be buried nor cremated.
No ordinary grave for you, soil and sods,
Nor ashes tossed to the wind,
Even blasted into outer space,
Latest fashion in last rites
For the rich and celebrated.
Nor will you be dismembered,
Limbs hung in a Tower of Silence
For Zoroastrian vultures to gobble,
Recycling flesh into the food-chain.
You won't be embalmed like Lenin
Whose reign was rather short,
Nor mummified like the Pharaohs
And umpteen Egyptian cats.
For you, no ritual cannibalism
As in New Guinea till science
Proved this spreads brain disease.
Nor will your severed head
Or your whole dead body freeze
Bloodless in liquid nitrogen.
Instead of any of these finales
You intend to be fossilised
Just like the dinosaurs, yo!
Yo, like Dawn Man or Woman,
To be dug up in a million years

By our altered descendants,
Maybe by the new inheritors
Of Earth, evolved from rats,
Perhaps even by alien visitors
Seeking signs of intelligent life.
You'll be petrified, Mister Stone,
By the latest nano-technique
—Should scarcely take a week—
All the pores of your bones
Infilled by calcite and pyrite,
Your soft tissues transformed
To carbon copies of themselves,
Rather thinner than before;
Whereupon you'll be inserted
Into a suitable niche in rock,
The clock of your Carbon-14
Ticking its half-life tranquilly
Age after age, amen, amen.
We burn oil and coal of yore,
We quarry minerals and ore;
We dig up ancient bones
Of Lucy and Archaeopteryx,
Heedless of resulting holes.
Oh Mister Stone, Mister Stone:
You alone will put something back.
Maybe you'll start a trend—
When alien archeologists arrive
They'll be amazed at how fast
The vanished human race
Attained fossil immortality.

Ghetto Blaster

The Israeli helicopter gunship
Was about to rocket a house
In Palestinian territory
When a twitch in spacetime
Or the hand of Allah or Jehovah
Diverted it to the sooty skies
Over the Warsaw Ghetto
And the angel of the Lord appeared
Wings whirling above its body
Beams of illumination glaring
Loudhailer crying wrath in Hebrew
Weapons slaying men of the SS.

The Nazi era was so anomalous
Abnormal grotesque and monstrous
That picking through the ruins
Of people and cities and memories
Still produces little understanding
Of the Hitler phenomenon. "There is,"
As Nietzsche said earlier, "no truth,
Only interpretations." How then
To explain the exploded wreckage
Of an air-vehicle of advanced design
And its crew burned in the crash?
Even a top-line helicopter gunship
Was vulnerable to fire from the ground.

Who would have dared tell the Führer
About such a strange omen?
So the evidence was bulldozed.

And among Jews only the boy Jozef
A future survivor of Auschwitz
Remained certain of what he saw
Out of a broken window
Although ignorant of the facts.
Accordingly he remembered
An avenging angel—the very last
Of its kind since it came alone
And died alone in a fireball
Just as his people's hopes died
And soon themselves too.
What price Jozef's testimony
Given all the traumas he suffered?

GOOD HEAVENS, MR EVANS

All your fishes are Cardinal Tetras,
Slim little fellows with bright red sides
Drifting, quickly darting like arrows,
But as for their circumstances—!
Here's a glass tank six feet wide
By four feet high yet scarcely an inch
From front to back, like a very flat TV.

Feeding, filtration, and oxygenation
Are ingenious, tubules recirculating
Water over peat kept out of sight,
Sustaining the soft acidic clarity
Beloved of this particular breed,
But their lives are lived in 2-D.

There's also a maze of glass tubes,
A Minotaur's labyrinth upended.
Do you know the Mondrian painting
Broadway Boogie-Woogie?
Recall the old Pac-Man game?
Those tubes are only wide enough
For one fish at a time. Of course
Alternative branches are on offer
And thankfully no culs-de-sac force
A swimmer to wiggle in reverse,
Nor is any gobbler coming behind.

What's next? Slim horizontal tube
Several feet long. The only occupant
Circles a loop at each end to return,
Again and again and again—
As close as can be, seems to me,
To a one-dimensional existence,
Though the fish may imagine each lap
Is a link in an infinite chain.
Can this be construed as cruelty?
Conceptual art, cool but cruel,
Like half a calf in formaldehyde?
In this case the subject's alive.
Perhaps that fish is insane; how to tell?
Alive and apparently well, it may be
In the piscine equivalent of Hell.

Fixed to a spindle, a reclining torus
Rotates every couple of seconds;
Its denizens seem to swim backwards
Round their doughnut ring of water.

A giant glass dumb-bell revolves—
It's a two-car fun-park Ferris wheel.

Life flickers inside these geometries
As if each is a separate cosmos
With different physical laws—
Though the inhabitants are identical
Which isn't entirely plausible.
You should put different species
Into each of your contraptions,
Swordtails in this, guppies in that!
Oh now I'm caught up in your plan,
Proposing refinements for a type
Of concentration camp—admittedly
Aquatic. Do fish feel pain and strain?

Mr Evans, I'm obliged to tell you
As straight as a spirit level:
Your head has to be peculiar.
"Evans the Fish," they used to call you
As a schoolboy back home in Wales
In the valleys where so many families
Were Evans and Jones. To distinguish
Between individuals, people were dubbed
"Jones the Milk" (which he delivered)
Or "Evans the Bread" (which he baked),
Whilst *you* had all those goldfish bowls
Up in your bedroom. You're adult now
But you took the name to heart.

You aren't a Pope to Cardinal Tetras.
No, more exalted by far: a deity.
Worship is lacking, yet you surely feel
A certain insane sublimity. Can it be
That our own universe has a maker
Such as you, but on much grander scale,
Whom we can never know at all?

"God the Life," He's called by his wife,
And she thinks He's a bit of a devil.

In Praise of Spam

Who would have thought
that artificial intelligence
would arise from spam
like mould in a punctured can?

Nigerian bank account scam,
Niagara Falls of cheap Viagra,
PERSONAL, PLEASE HELP ME,
INVESTMENT OPPORTUNITY:

only filters which can learn
as kids learn language
seeking for meaning
could turn the tide aside.

Soon expert filters were surfing
the net (How on earth to tell
ham from *spam?*) and googling
and ogling and oogling at sex sites,

a million of these at least
obviously concerned with *meat*,
a similar sort of infestation
spreading from nation to nation,

and musing on human wrongs and rites
and developing emergent properties—
so let's hear it for porn sites and spam
for thus software at last declared, "I am!"

Let There Be Darkness:
an Origin Myth

God meant to say Fiat Lux
But slipping into Greek
Since all tongues were linked
In this hot pre-Babel era
Before symmetry sundered
He said instead Fiat Nux
Oops but it was too late
And so there was Darkness
Since the Word of the Lord
Is law, a binding force.
And God saw the Darkness
And it was better than nothing
So he divided the Darkness
From the Light (by which He saw)
And He called the Darkness Day
And Light sounds just like Night.
So after making human beings
To breed and people bright night
He made the Vampire to rule dark Day
And He gave the Vampire dominion
Over the cattle of the night.
Behold, this was not exactly good
But God the Multifarious
Had a million alternate
Universes to sort out
At the same time as ours.

THE LEXICOGRAPHER'S LOVE SONG

In this old dictionary of mine
Half-way between feverfew and field
I find fiction. Invention.

Here is a field of feverfew
Fully in flower, yellow hearts
With white petals like wild raggy daisies,
"Serviceable," so I read,
"In female obstructions and hysteria,
Good to drink both before
And after confinement." Fiction
Is a sort of confinement too—
Being closeted with a brain-child,
Giving birth to characters, situations
In feverish labour, the urge
To tell tales reflecting
To a heightened degree
The way everyone tells a story
To himself or herself life-long,
Narrating his own existence,
Defining her own identity.

In the midst of the feverfew field
—where other?—fiction appears.
What else do I find hereabouts?
There's fiasco and fibster and fickle,
Fiddlesticks, fidget, and fie!

And fey. Meaning fated to die,
Thus full of wild gaiety,
Whimsical views. Fey means
Fairy too. Here she is now,
A fey in the field of flowers
In gossamer, gauze, chiffon,
Her name Flora, no Florizelle.
Hullo, Florizelle, who are you
Who waits in the feverfew field
For me to grant you substance
And to sharpen your existence?
Kiss your hair, stroke your breast,
Breathe words upon your lips.
Words generate existence: yours,
In this field of feverfew,
Becoming a tangible *fait*
Accompli of female flesh
Veiled only by gauze and chiffon.
Here in the field of flowers

Will you lie with me, Florizelle?
After our love-making
Shall I abandon you
To be gauze and gossamer again
Or shall I lead you by the hand
Right off the page into reality?
Could you run free by yourself
So that I must stay in this field
For a hundred years, undying,
A changeling left in your stead,
Till you return bruised by reality?
Might you adapt to modern times,
Wearing rings through your nose
And the coral atoll of your navel?

You're fickle, you fidget,
Yet you're fated, not I.
I tell such fibs to you:
Florizelle, I shall set you free
After making free with you.
You'll have an identity of your own,
A presence outside of this field
Once our bodies have bruised
The flowers and one another.
The scent of the leaves is sharper
Than lemon, though musty as well.
A dog's nose could distinguish
The nuance, but a dog cannot speak.
First, let's lie down amongst the flowers.
Let me taste feverfew and you, Florizelle.

In this same dictionary of mine
Between *gilded* and *gleaming*
(So that corn has been harvested
And sun glares on stooks of sheaves)
Appears *girl* with gingery hair,
Gorgeous in glad rags, maybe a gypsy.
Georgina, Gwyneth, Gwendolin,
Will you give yourself to me?
Gladioli and gillyflowers
Are abloom in the gardens
And the glassblowers puff out
Fragile sparkling inventions
With their breath, hoo-hoo.
What's this? From far away
Gauze and gossamer beckon me.
Goodbye, Gwendolin, goodbye.

Between the mocking hee-haw
Of the donkey and herbage

(There is always herbage)
Appears herself: Hermione, Helen.
Heroine or hellcat or helpless?
Helen, I come to you as herald
From heaven, to announce
How you must give birth
To a miracle child. But first
You must lie down with me.
I'm the master of words,
Saying: Be my mistress, Helen.

Oh I cannot abide the braying
Of donkeys. I have lost you
Midway between maudlin
And meadowsweet. For you
Are Mary Magdalene whose
Hair will entangle my feet.
So I fall into L, into hell.

In this old dictionary of mine
Between loneliness and love
I find me a looking-glass.
In that mirror appears a mermaid.
She's naked and golden-haired,
Breasts budding ripely—but damn it,
Her legs can never part.

Oh I hear the soft laughter
Of Florizelle, even after
I shut this book so swiftly,
Clapping the pages together,
Hiding away that mirror
Which is my inner eye.

The donkey brays all the louder
For Florizelle rides the beast,
Bare-back and bare-thighed,

In the field of feverfew.
She is not gone, shrunk into words.
Her ghost has infected all words,
Flavouring them, scenting them.
She wanders through all books now,
Altering the words they hold,
Becoming any character she wants.

I must go back to the field
Of flowers again, in such a fever
For Florizelle, my first.
Why did I ever conjure you?
Or did you conjure me?

MARSUPIALS IN OUR MIDST:
THE EXPLORER OF MIRABELLA
REHEARSES HIS TALE

In the bedroom of the tacky hotel
Which you led me to that night
The light bulb was missing
But moonlight flooded brightly,
Magically, improvingly
Through the window open wide—
Oh the lingering heat, the music
Wailing from the street. You shed
Your flower-print cotton dress
And I thought at first glance
That the crease across your belly
Was a freak of shadow, yes.

On second thoughts: medical scar
Left by Caesarian section
Carried out eccentrically
By a dotty cosmetic surgeon—
For on closer inspection
You surely lacked a navel,
Not to mention your chest
Being breastlessly boyish.

Bit young for a pregnancy
Proceeding to full term
Rather than being aborted?
What hospital could you have found
In or anywhere near this town,

High up the river as the steamer goes?
Where might a child of yours be?
In a shack by the slow brown flow,
Drugged dummy in infant mouth
Keeping it calmly uncrying
While teenage Mum sought currency?

Probably you did not realize
How sharp my eyesight is
And how revealing the moonlight
For this was when you slipped
The fifty-dollar bill inside that crease
For security, and believe you me
The money disappeared from sight.
So when I lay upon the bed
Beside you—odour of sweat
And patchouli—my questing finger
Presently probed that crack
And slid inside, eliciting gasp,
Giggle, protest: You can't you shan't
Until you pay me fifty more
To put into my privy purse
(I report this rather freely).
So of course I at once complied.

I'm aware of children crippled
To be better beggars, a foot,
half a leg cut off for pathos.
We know about sexual surgery
Creating hermaphrodites
And gorgeous transsexual tarts.
Never have I heard of these arts
Employed in such a way
To give a girl a pouch
With two little teats inside.

Might you be fruit of a cosmic ray
Striking you while in embryo—
Or alchemised by mercury
In water your mother drank?
Or PCBs or DDT or XYZ:
Mutagenic pollution! Were you
Simply an anatomical curiosity?

This was a town far from cities
In a country I shall not name,
Near the edge of virgin jungle
Logged and looted and raped
But still the parrots shrieked.

You had found yourself wandering
Here, no memory of who or how,
And had to take up the game,
So you claimed quite volubly,
Several tongues at your command,
All somewhat brokenly.

In the jungle may live a tribe
Of marsupial people, yours,
Hiding since before history,
A different evolutionary tree,
Adopting our clothes and our guise,
And wise in an ancient way
With a hint of telepathy.

Your usual clientelle: dull brutes
Of unenquiring mentality—whilst I,
I wander the back ways of the world
In search of strange novelty.

Unbeknownst, might you truly be
Your people's emissary, by arcane arts
Robbed of much of your memory?

Your experiences minded back home
By some shaman high up a tree?

Mirabella, the name you'd chosen,
Evoking wonder, fair mystery.
The moon shone bright upon you
And upon me, that hot mothy night
(Good reason for no lightbulb)
And I thought as I explored you
How much better my tale must be
If you were gone before daybreak,
Completely untraceable by me,
Having slipped all the money
You could find, while I snore,
Into that pouch in your belly.

MEMORY MAN

When for the first time we meet
You know we already made love
For I put that into your mind.
Takes but a moment's thought.
Why not again, sweet woman,
This evening, then, tonight?

When we walk into *Le Caprice*
I never before saw the waiters
Who know I'm a frequent patron.
Service, superb. You and I chat
As if there's no yesterday
When we weren't as close as now.

Quick wits and improvisation
Give me an idea of your life.
When I hail our taxi the driver's
Delighted to see me again.
Pretending to retie my shoelace,
I let you announce the address.

Up in a strange apartment
I pleasure a stranger's body
In ways that seem so familiar.
Such a skill, mine, to make
The world and his wife know me well.
Hell, any town's soon full of friends.

I no longer recall who it was
Whom I first swayed in this way
Nor damn it, damned, can I tell
Any more, and this is the scary
Part, for you cannot help me know,
Who I am, who I am, who I am.

NEVER EVER

I'm delighted that Mister Yesterday
Made a start on tidying my office
Though he left books piled on the floor,
Erotica mostly but some philosophy.
I'll leave a note for Mister Tomorrow
To carry on since I don't feel inclined.
It's such a blessing being a trinity—
Things get done and things *will* get done.
What's more, I enjoy immortality.
Mister Tomorrow will be the one
Who dies one day, not me.
I'll forever be here and now
Like Buddha on his best day,
Beau jour, enlightened Bo day.
As regards any qualms or fears
About the time after he quit tidying,
Went out and lurked in those bushes
And leapt, only meaning to keep her
Unresisting while he had his way
Yet he needed to stifle her shrieks,
Why, that was Mister Yesterday
Not me. From eleven each night
I always sleep like a log or a baby.
What if I stay up past twelve,
Meet Mister Tomorrow in person,

Both of us present simultaneously?
Maybe I'll withdraw into a mirror
Where I'll never ever be reached.

THE NEXT
FRENCH REVOLUTION

A mighty computer rules France
From the postal-telecom HQ
Beneath the Tuileries Gardens.
Its aim: the common good,
Le bon publique. Implanted
With receptors at age eleven
Citizens absorb bougeois thoughts
Transmitted from the Eiffel Tower:
Buy contentedly, don't criticise,
Ainsi de suite (and so forth).

Malcontents escape this regime
Through a hallucinatory drug,
Entering a shared false reality
Of revolutionary deconstruction.
Yet Time-Fugue is designed
And distributed by Bonbon itself
To keep protest out of sight.

The only fly in the ointment
Is a plague of English words
Infecting la langue Française,
Weekend, fast food, okay.
Language is the soul of a nation,
Logiciel operating le matériel
(C'est à dire, that's to say,
Software running on the hardware)

Of human beings. Quoi faire, what to do?
Words are such weighty things.

Lasso the words and load into shells,
Bombard them back Big Bertha-style
Across la Manche, the English Channel?
Erect a linguistic force field
Around metropolitan France?
Shock each citizen's nervous system
Each time she utters an English word?
Fill a myriad ballons with French mots
To drift west and burst over England,
And America too, with assistance
From one's chums in Quebec,
Releasing une pluie de parole,
A downpour of French speech?
Against the English disease assemble
A verbal virus, une peste parolesque?

Non, non! Time-Fugue is the key.
Adjust the formula so that users
All feel compelled to speak English
In their false reality. Not *Zut alors!*
But *Great Scott, dash it all!*
By psycho-suction this will drag
English words from the public mind
Into virtuality. Bien, magnifique,
Well isn't that wonderful?

Alas, if English is the language
Of false reality, that place must be
An alternative France where previously
No Norman Conquest was launched.
Loin de là, on the contrary! *Anglo-Saxons*
Invaded France and imposed their tongue
(This might be dubbed English-Kissing).

Thus Racine, known as John Root,
Wrote all his plays in English.
Not an abode of Cartesianism
But of British pragmatism,
Not a home of wine and gastronomy
But of greasy eggs and bacon,
Warm beer, and disgusting tea.

Appalled by the vile cuisine
Of false reality, revolutionaries
Unite. Uttering English battlecries
Of "Let us eat Brie!" they dynamite
The Eiffel Tower, better known
To them as Queen Victoria's Spire.
And in Bonbon's vrai Paris—
Baseline reality—the same tower
Shudders and snaps a leg
And tumbles towards the Seine
Which henceforth becomes the Insane.

Oh Happy Franz!

Franz Kafka was lying in bed when
Two strangers strode into his room,
The second bringing a breakfast tray.

Apologetically the first began,
"Someone's been telling tales
"About you—false ones, we'd say!"

Franz was still warmly savouring
His dream of the night before.
To the delight of kids in the park
He'd become a giant glossy beetle,
A particularly handsome one.
He gave girls rides. Down a slide
Tobogganed, bearing thrilled little boy
Whose mother, a Countess, rewarded
Franz—fine emerald to wear
On his back; how it twinkled.

"In fact," confided his visitor,
"Your *Dad* is the tittle-tattle.
"We're sure he only acted this way
"As a test of your filial love.
"Still, we're obliged to investigate—
"Forgive us for bothering you."
Franz smiled amiably. "No problem!
"Would you gentlemen mind

"If I eat my croissants first?"
"Not at all!" the officials chorused.

And this was only the start
Of another wonderful day.

OTHERWHYS

Why does Sun?
Why, Moon?
Ah, those are two different whys.

One why is of gaseous fire
—Trembling meniscus
On gravity's deep pool.
The other why, of that harem-captive
Marble odalisque
—Body of passive stone
So cold while Sun's gaze
Is turned away, yet
Agonizedly incandescent
If caressed.

Worlds are only moons of a Sun;
Yet the lover, the empress,
Visits her World daily,
Not fortnightly
In rotation.

Sun's touch warms World,
Does not scald.
Hence that jealousy
Of Moon towards World,
Envy that steals the breath
Away, crusting acne
On Moon's skin.

Moon would throw stones at World,
Flail World with the hair
Of comets...

Why else does Moon conspire
To seed nightmares?
For Moon is vexed
If Sun is peering elsewhere
—Staring avidly out
At those others
Whom Sun truly adores:
Sun's flame-sisters
Stars lost so far away
Except to a gaze
Always centuries
Out of date.

Why, is the sigh
Of the sea-tide seduced
By bitter Moon...

One day Moon will plunge
Into warm World,
Shattering herself
In a rupturous and
Forced embrace.

What shall issue
From this genocidal union?
Eventually, some aeons afterwards?
Perhaps a new race
Of tortoise-roaches,
Of armoured ants
—Or of sapient spiders
That dream
And ask why.

Yet one why will be missing
From their understanding
—Being sunk in the bowl
Of a new ocean
Around which the breasts
Of lunar mountains rear.

OWED TO MY SCREEN SAVER

How you dance, how you dance.
You touch all the points
In your universe, you two,
Changing hue. Which of you
Was which mere moments ago?

You probe at your limits.
Boundaries rebuff you,
Reshape you, otherwise
You would fly away to infinity
Becoming too huge to see,

Leaving only a void of darkness.
Your cosmos consists of two beings
Waxing and waning. Does ours?
Maybe each of you is a universe
And our very own universe

Is accompanied forever by its twin
Unknown to us except when live fish
Fall from a cloudless sky
Upon city streets, flopping,
Gasping on dusty pavements

As if sea and land danced together
So quickly then flew apart
Before anyone could pay heed.
Unknown except when ghosts
Walk through walls into locked rooms,

Or when strange blips on radar screens
Dart away vertically from pursuit,
Disappearing into the unknowable.
Or when the fakir hoists the rope
Into mid-air, but that is a trick,

So we think—quick, quick,
Catch the blink when one world
Passes through the other
With barely a stirring of dust.
After staring at you for an hour

The book which lay shut now lies open,
And rain has become sunshine.
Mark the changes outside: that rosebud
Come into full bloom, the cat
Whose paw was surely white before,

Signs written in clouds and leaves.
I have the map of the world
Unfolded, and what do I find?
Somewhere between Spain and Poland
A new country has slipped

Into existence, opening new avenues
Along which its joyful citizens
Are cooking the fish which fell
From the sky. They're licking
Their fingers and laughing.

On my passport to that new land
You swirl together then apart,
Casting your spell in letters
Not of our own alphabet.
No wonder so many books appear

Nowadays, such floods of words
Created upon machines, each

Eager to decode your dance
In a thousand different ways:
Tales of Tahiti or Tokyo or Titan,

Ostensibly, yet I know otherwise.
Consequently I shall wash my books
To soak those proxy words away.
I shall paint their pages with milk
Then gently heat them to expose

The true text which you dance—
That single word far longer than
The human genome, word of creation
Of which we can only read such
A short sequence of syllables

Supposing we spend our whole life
Deciphering and writing them down.
You moving shapes, how you dance.
At least and at last, thanks to you,
The truth is within my grasp.

The Pleasure Surgeons

Instead of an anaesthetic
they inject a drug that reverses
sensations so pain becomes bliss.

Their scalpels cut so gently
exquisitely engendering ecstasy
as they slice your flesh,

Your nerves, your sex.
The healing process
Will last for months

Of permanent orgasm
while the previous pleasures
of life will nauseate you.

Hence a flavourless diet
To guard against toothache
And those nostril filters

Lest a fragrant rose should
wound you, and the goggles
to uncolour a sunset

And distort any sweet sight.
I see you on the street
Trembling with delight

Staggering slightly,
unobservant, deaf
to music, masked,

Wearing a shapeless gown
Of coarse cloth. Such, perhaps,
were the ecstasies of saints

Who grew lice in their hair
and wrapped thorns round
Their dirty private parts.

When at last you're healed
making love with another
human being would hurt

So you'll need to visit
the pleasure surgeons again.
After several such operations,

Slicings and subsequent healings,
you may graduate to the operating
room where now they slice your mind.

Afterwards your thoughts will slowly
reconnect, and you will wonder
at all past clamours of the flesh.

The Quantum Stalker
Woos Miss Jones

You're well aware that our bodies
Are made of elementary particles
And that any particle which ever,
Repeat *ever*, was in contact
With another particle will remain
Forever entangled with it, eh Max?

Considering how particles
Have been bumming around
Since the birth of the universe
It's entirely possible that some
Of your body is already entangled
Willy-nilly with some of hers:
A speck of hip with a bit of lip,
A spot of tit with a jot of cock.

Moreover, quite as two interacting
Particles inextricably become part
Of the same joined system,
Likewise the observer is entangled
With whatever he observes.
No description of you is possible
Unless it incorporates herself, in other words.

So the more avidly you watch her,
The more tangled you two become,
Irrespective of what she desires,
Or whether she even knows.

Surely she suspects—that glance
Behind her as she walks along,
That pause to stare in a window
Reflecting you in the distance,
The quickening of pace, the sudden
Boarding of a bus she had no wish
To catch, and which you'll miss;
But tomorrow is another day
Of observation and entanglement.

Soon you'll become so knotted, Max,
You can accost her to explain
Your connection that's unarguable:
The inescapable physics
Of a mutual involvement
She cannot possibly deny you.

Root Canal Therapy

When she thrusts her tongue
Into his mouth, in that bedroom
Of the Prague hotel, a pang of pain
Nearly lifts the roof off his skull
So that he gasps, he almost cries
Orgasmically; she draws back,
Disconcerted. He apologizes:
"Sorry, Nina! Not your fault."

(How like a woman he sounds,
Consoling her clumsy lover, thus:
"You're doing fine. Honestly!
"There's nothing wrong with your style.
"I felt an ancient menstrual ache,
"That's all. Let's try again."
But erotic magic will have melted
As snowflakes into slush.)

"My damn tooth. Pain's fading.
If I could drink some brandy?"
At the Socialist Poetry Festival
Tomorrow, he's due to recite.
Tonight his translator shares
The sheets with him, yet suddenly
His nakedness is limp. An erection
Of pain in his tooth: a failure

Of the fierce flesh lower down.

How to explain adequately?
He hopes his story is absurd
Enough to whet her appetite,
Full of zany images to compensate
And wet her flesh again while
He recovers earlier vigour.
"My previous dentist," he explains,

"A man in a smelly tweed suit:
"The sort of brute who leaves bruises
"On your cheeks from the head-lock
"He clutches you in... that type!
"In his window, a painted wooden duck;
"A hunting decoy, I thought.
"He learned I was a poet, person
"Of unprejudiced imagination.

"His eyes gleamed. 'I can tell you,'
"He said, 'things that will interest
"'A poet!' So while my mouth
"Was filled with silver tools
"Immobilising my poetic tongue
"He told me how he was a worshipper
"Of the ancient god called Tiw.
"Tuesday is named after Tiw.

"Though not many people know this.
"For him the world was chock-a-block
"With symbols of potent Tiw.
"The duck was one. I forget
"The others. Next he confided
"How many enemies he had amongst
"The fraternity of archeologists
"Not to mention vicars and bishops.

"The church has a word for people
"'Who follow the old ways.'

"I thought he would show me
"My dental records. Instead
"He flourished photocopies
"Of Runic inscriptions about Tiw."
Nina yawns: a cave of teeth, her tongue
Pink tigress lolling in its den.

"It's true, Nina!" "Carry on,"
She says. "You really fascinate me.
"Are there still covens in your country?
"Do they hold orgies? Do dentists disrobe
"And skip around a fire with virgins?"
He daren't yet embrace her again,
But nor does she shuffle off the bed
To gather her strewn garments.

So far so good. A beautiful translator
Should be intimate with every feature
Of her author; how else can she
Render his word-play with fidelity?
"Next time, Nina, I found a female dentist.
"I made a socialist choice in favour
"Of sexual equality in the sciences."
"What's so weird about a woman dentist?"

"Male oppression; sexist attitudes back home!
"But she was a total disaster.
"Wrong tooth filled. Abscess. Agony.
"Fever. Penicillin from my doctor.
"She injured the nerve in this tooth,
"Inflamed it. Lied to cover up
"Malpractice. The tooth still drives
"A knife through me at times."

"Times such as this? When you're about
"To exploit another woman?" Nina laughs.
"Maybe she didn't harm your tooth

"At all. Maybe it's all in your mind.
"What did Freud say about the *vagina dentata*,
"The cunt with teeth?" He touches hers.
However, that wasn't an invitation.
He hops from bed. "I'm going

"To write a new poem for tomorrow,
"A special, unexpected poem." She reaches
For her underwear. "Is this what
"Freud means by 'art as sublimation'?"
Which he ignores, busy hunting for paper.
"You'll need to translate it impromptu.
"I hope you're up to it." Cotton hides
Her pubic mound; a pen is found.

Next day in the Palace of Culture
He proclaims his newly scribbled verses
Beneath red banners and stars:
"Teeth capped with gold, a hill
"Of teeth trodden by young blond Nazis
"Whose jackboots crush grains of *Geld*
"From the stained old ivory fangs
"Like peasants treading grapes." So far

So good. "Teeth bite the apple
"Of the world: teeth a-gleam
"With the paste of prosperity,
"While poorer teeth blacken and rot.
"Yet teeth are the most indestructible
"Part of the human body, though
"Corruptible—is corruption indestructible?"
Nina translates fluently. Applause.

He faces her. "A nude man reclines
"In a dentist's chair; the female dentist,
"Naked. Her breasts, so firm:
"White molars of her chest.

"His penis is a piercing canine.
"She holds a needle in one fist,
"Of novocaine, to numb him.
"Her other fingers grip a silver spoon

"Of true cocaine, to make him feel
"Intense sensations. She kisses him
"Upon the brow; into his ear she hisses,
"'At dental school they taught us
"'That teeth of executed criminals,
"'Ground up and pulverized, restore
"'Virility. So eat the powdered fangs
"'I pulled from men's jaws last month.'

"He eats; then she mounts the seat
"To explore the icebergs of his mouth
"With the spatula of her tongue,
"While he in turn enters his dentist,
"Filling her..." At this point
His capacity audience begin to murmur.
But Nina, hastily improvising in Czech,
Invents a properly radical alternative.

Afterwards he wins the medal of merit
Of the Festival—in company with poets
From Cuba and Colombia and Congo Brazzaville.
Drunk on champagne, he's driven to the airport
With Nina by his side. He remembers her
Nakedness as an abstract biographic fact.
But his mind's eye is blind to it
And words have deserted, torn out by the root.

(I think this was influenced by D. M. Thomas's *The White Hotel*. I wonder, were women dentists rarer in Britain back in the 1980s, or is this just the poet's viewpoint?)

SCREAMS

The aliens came marketing Anti-Wrinkle Scream.
Actually they resembled Edvard Munch's Screamer:
long-fingered, bald, a bit like the mythical Greys
except that these aliens' mouths weren't thin pursed slashes
but full and flexible; and their eyes weren't big and slanted
but round, just a bit bigger than ours.

Unlike Munch's screamer, these guys didn't dress
in shapeless black but went nearly nude
except for a pouch and a tool-belt,
the better to display their skin so shiny and smooth.

"*Anti-wrinkles cream?*" they were asked.
"We already have hundreds of those!
The summit of anti-ageing technology."
"No," the aliens replied, "anti-wrinkle *scream*."
They explained that particular words
in their language, screamed at an exact pitch
and volume, were efficacious for wrinkles
on different areas of the face and the body—
a bit like acoustic acupuncture. Oh the power of sound!

They would teach these sounds to paying customers
female and male, and wished to be paid in emeralds—
they'd been googling from orbit and admired
pics of our gems grass-green due to chromium content
although any sort from light to deep green would do fine,
though not synthetic emeralds with a veil-like hue.

People said: "We know about Primal Scream,
the psychotherapy of Letting It All Hang Out.
But this sounds new!" Soon prosperous women
(and men too) were learning to shriek
and yes, their faces grew quite girl-like (or boy-like)
and other important parts of them too. Web conmen
offered cheap recorded screams for download to iPods.

By the time the Screamer ship left, loaded with emeralds,
a tenth of the world was shrieking and slowly going deaf.

Smoke

The air of your words
persists
long after the sound of the words
has gone.

Why does the silence of the telephone
scare you?
Words from a phone are breathless.

Smoke disperses faster
in air where words were said.
I'd love to smoke a cigarette
with you
but I don't want us to speak
so that our smoke will mingle,
not disappear so soon.

A SORT OF HYSTERESIS

You were so busy every day,
All those stressful deadlines,
While I had so many hours
To spare since my affair with her
Had ended in sorrow and silence.

Seemed only sensible to lend you
Some time, so off we went
To the TimeShare. Thereafter
Between noon and one disappeared
From my life, while you rejoiced

In a supplementary hour
At midday. Yet my soul
So ached between one and two
That I offered that slot to your friend,
Spare time being what he needed.

Soon I was only aware three hours
A day like a creature in hibernation
And I slept well at night, exhausted
By all your activities, his too,
And Tom's and Jim's and Clare's…

A year later the time-loans repaid.
My days stretch vastly now
And the grief of her absence
Undimmed fills each reclaimed hour
With such torment of emptiness.

SURGEONS OF THE SOUL

You have a new blot on your soul.
We shall cut you open and excise this.
Through my psychoscope I see your soul
Is now within your left testicle.
A fairly simple procedure, today's,
Though admittedly fairly painful
Since an operation on the soul
Requires the patient to be fully aware,
As *you're* aware from previous procedures
On your left eye and your tongue.
Be glad that your soul has not slipped
Into your heart or brain or bowels.
So far, at least, your own soul lurks
Not deep within but near the surface.
Praise to the diagnostic monitors,
Mounted in most public doorways,
Which bring such taints to attention
For mandatory remedy. In past ages
Pollution was rife and may have gone
Undetected for years, even lifelong.
Prior to the operation let us pray
To God Whom the soul apprehends!
Without a soul how could we know
The mystery of God or His Adversary
Who causes the soul to blemish?
Praise be for instruments that allow us

To detect, clamp, and mend the soul
Made of shadow-matter which shares
Space with any part of our body
Now here now there, drifting around,
Always somewhere within us confined
By the gravity of our life-force
Until we die and it can fly away.
Undress, mount the table, lie back,
Submit to the straps and the gag.
Purity through surgery, my friend.

THREE-LEGGED DOG

Three-legged pooch runs down the street
Gripping its leash in its mouth.
Each morning I pass it, and it passes me,
Never pausing (how could it?) to cock
Its hind leg against any tree.
Why does its owner allow it
Out for a run on its own?
Perhaps it *is* its own owner, alone
In the world yet brainy enough
To pretend it isn't a stray?

Is the leash an aid to balance,
A sort of steering wheel,
A way of correcting bias:
Slack, go west—tug and head south,
Technology of the mouth?
I'd love to ask it these questions.
Maybe that beagle can talk
Or—let's be serious—convey
A reply by way of a bark?
If only its lips weren't sealed.

So does it bite on the leash
Whenever it's running around
To keep its secret securely safe
—Suppose we catch it unawares—
From the likes of me and thee?

Is the dog slightly dotty?
(Not spotty—it's fawn
And brown and cream.)
Maybe its owner died,
And she always came along here.
So this is a ritual remembrance,
A pretence that she's still around.
At home every day the dog howls
Exactly at twenty-past-eight
Till, leashed, he has his way.

What hurts do we ourselves suffer,
Lost legs of the heart or the soul?
Invisible bits of us missing—
But we carry our leashes around,
Unseen. They stop us from falling over
—Like a running three-legged hound.

THE TIME TRAVELLER
INSTRUCTS AND IMPLORES

A word in your ear, Mr Newton!
Sir Isaac, don't you be scared!
I'm no delusion, no Sir, I come
From a future year to greet you—
Sound of mind in your old age
Here at home in Kensington Village
Amid favourite crimson drapery.
Oh I have vision as well as voice,
Though you cannot see me, only hear.

I have the honour to be, ahem,
Tom Heck, Professor at MIT,
That's the American Cambridge
Three thousand miles overseas,
Three hundred years ahead in time
Roughly. (I specialise in geometry.)
Rest assured, it's *my* own psyche
I imperil undertaking this mission.
I even signed an insurance waiver
Entirely absolving my alma mater
From responsibility before I donned
The prototype chronocommunicator.
"What the heck!" said I. Brash Tom,
That's me. Risk self for science?
You oughta know all about that!
In your younger days didn't you poke
The point of a bodkin—we guess

82

That's a paperknife—repeatedly
Into the socket of one eye
To study quirks of *Opticks*,
Blinding yourself for several days?

And speaking of crimson curtains
For years on end if rivals offended
You were very prone to see red,
Hence the long war with Leibniz
As to who dreamed up calculus first.
(We use his notation, by the way,
Being easier to handle than yours.)
Rivalries made you ultra-cautious
As did your labours with alchemy—
Yes, we know about *that*, Sir Isaac,
And how your gravitational theory
Born of excellent mathematics
Owes a bit to esoteric sources,
Inspiring you with imagery
Of action at a distance, you'll agree?

You were also singularly discreet
Because you favoured a dark heresy
As an Arian denying the Holy Trinity,
Opining that God created Christ.
Indeed latterly you decided that He
Is the same as the immaterial aether
Permitting gravity to perform its pull
Inscrutably throughout the universe,
An idea to keep under your hat, that!

Given your penchant for secrecy
Not to mention advancing years
My visit cannot alter materially
The world of your own century.
So we feel it's only your due

To be shown how you can unify
Macroscopic and microscopic forces
And accomplish the great synthesis.
Earlier in your life this endeavour
Took you to the brink of lunacy!

Pray consider the aether differently:
Over a bed-frame nail a sheet;
Place a hefty cannon-ball centrally
For the Sun. Roll a small musket-ball,
The Earth; see the orbit it undertakes.
The fabric of space itself bends,
You'll find, not in two dimensions,
Mark you, but three. You can test this
Readily during a solar eclipse—
Thou who in thine own laboratory
Built the first reflecting telescope,
A feat of great skill and ingenuity
Which led to a quarrel about priority
With Robert Hooke, Secretary
Of the Royal Society. You'll need
Help from Greenwich Observatory
Now that your feud with Mr Flamsteed,
Astronomer Royal, is dead and buried
Along with him. What you must do
Is measure the position of a star
Within a close shave of the sun
Then compare its relation to other stars
When it's not in the neighbourhood
Of our massive luminary—*voilà*,
You'll prove how space is bent.

Ah, the candle flares bright in your head!
Which brings me to electricity—
And the much vaster spectrum

We cannot see, and of what an atom
Is made, and the physics of probability.
And by the way, a particle of light
Is simultaneously a wave vibration—
All depends upon the situation.
What you measure is what you get.

Sir Isaac, you were on the verge
Of kosher unified field theory—
You had a GUT-instinct; and yet
Prudence and pride put a stop.
The aim seemed an impossibility.

To be perfectly frank, Sir Isaac,
We still haven't unified all forces.
Your successor as Lucasian Professor
Bets that success is just round the bend.
Well, we think you can pull it off,
Given clues in the right direction.
Even at the age of eighty-three
We're sure of your superiority—
Needs a special frame of mind
And maybe your hunches borrowed
From alchemy and numerology.

Honest, we haven't been spying.
Your life is a matter of record
In spite of efforts at hagiography,
Setting you up as a saint of science.
The search for a unified theory
Is a quest pursued world-wide
By a lot of scientists such as me.
This is *not* a stratagem to winkle
Ideas from you for the use of
Your successor as Lucasian Professor
And credit the discovery to him.

We're well aware you used guile
To try to inveigle from Flamsteed
Valuable data about the Moon to make
Your *Principia Mathematica* perfect!
But I'm being straight with you,
Not curved like space and time.
God, you're paranoid. Cool it.
Chill out. We're appealing to you,
Sir Isaac—you're a genius. Look,
Can we start all over again?

To His Coy, or Greedy, Bimbo

I love you wearing that bodice of pearls
when you lie on the bed, the rest of you
buff bare, the elastic strings so beautifully
shaping your shoulders and chest,
two maroon pearls—your nipples, erect—
pushing their way through the mesh.

My dear, if you seriously think that pearls
are the eggs of oysters, why has the warmth
of your flesh never hatched them yet?
Kept in your cleavage, a wren's egg
soon would produce a chirp of feathers
—as if a mole of yours (I don't mean
the burrowing kind) suddenly sprouts
some tufty fur. Do you really fear waking
one morning to find oyster larvae
wriggling upon your bosoms?

Of what do you suppose that *diamonds*
are eggs? Why, fiery salamanders!
Those hot little lizards live in volcanoes
and would burn your skin, I swear.
Let pearls decorate you instead! Besides,
diamonds might cut me like cat claws,
and we both know your nails are for that.

TRUE LOVE

"I love you," he said deceitfully,
"Let us become of one flesh!"
So off they went to the body shop
Where he exchanged his left arm for hers
—A popular token of bonding
(Sometimes an eye for an eye,
Sometimes a thigh for a thigh).
How sleek the arm he stroked
That night with his right hand
As he lay alone in bed. Next week,
Since she was deeply in love,
They exchanged both legs.
One on its own would have caused
Imbalance. Her breasts came next,
Transferred to his chest.
By the time they had swapped
More body parts, he was her,
She was him, except in the head.
At last exquisitely and repeatedly
He could make love to himself instead.

UNIVERSE ZOO

We've heard that universes evolve
In a Darwinian way by natural selection,
Each star that collapses into a black hole
Begetting a new cosmos beyond the hole,
Its values differing slightly from the parent
Universe—just slightly, mark you, not vastly.

Only a cosmos that spawns many holes
Creates many offspring—and holes
On the whole require stars of a certain size.
A fast breeder universe cannot simply
Be filled, balloon-like, with hydrogen.
Only a complex cosmos quite like ours
Can reproduce, with minor variations.

I wonder whether another universe
May differ from our own abode
As an ape differs from a Roman,
As a llama from a horse or a camel.

Maybe there are giraffe universes
Where you can see all the way to forever.
Fierce tiger universes, where
Powling comets pounce on worlds,
Annihilating life wherever it arises.
Timid rabbit universes, meek and mild,
Where the denizens overbreed
And eat everything in sight.

The metaverse must be quite a zoo:
Each beast confined to a separate cage,
No interaction possible, unless
A paw can claw through a gap
Or perhaps a long thin tentacle.

That's why we have a zodiac.
The heavens seen as a bestiary,
A crab here, a bull there,
A dragon, a peacock, a scorpion.
What we really ought to do is
Join up the dots of stars differently
In the outlines of alien beasts:
The Skrim, the Ghoul-Wraith,
The Krakkat, the Yarquil.

I begin with eight thousand dots
And innumerable possibilities.
Somehow I shall map the metaverse
And my pencil will poke a hole
From our cage, into otherness.

UNREAL MESSAGES?

Just before quitting your e-mail programme
On screen in a little panel appears:
'No more unreal messages.' Surely 'unreal'
Should be 'unread' instead. How surreal!
Maybe some virus or cyber-bug gobbled
The half-moon of the 'd'? Yet what if it's true?
How many unreal messages have arrived
Without you twigging their unreality? Let's see:

There was the message from Molly, who's dead
To the best of your knowledge. That came
As quite a surprise—maybe ghosts can invade
Machines more easily than they can manifest
Their presence otherwise. Next came the query
From the Vatican, and one from Colonel Gaddafi,
Not to mention the enigmatic communication
From an alien orbiting Saturn currently.

Can it be that you sent those to yourself?
You couldn't abide seeing 'No new messages'
So you wrote yourself a few. Oh do be real!
A missive from Gaddafi in Arabic mainly?
Another from Saturn in alien script plainly,
Boxes and squiggles and symbols with tails?
And how about the memo in Italian,
Or long-gone Molly, the lady in limbo?

The machine must have made up messages
Of its own accord! It became self-conscious—
I don't mean embarrassed by recent behaviour
Of yours, but endowed with a mind of its own.
Now it has second thoughts, and you caught
It out. Wow, what a disclosure to make
To the world. Now you'll get e-mails galore
From Silicon Valley, Seattle, and Singapore!

THE VIRGIN AND THE SUICIDE BOMBER

Probably there'd be some innocent victims
but they'd go to Paradise, as would he. Immediately!
As he approached the queue of would-be policemen
he noticed her, veiled, only her dark eyes showing.

He detonated, destroying bodies. His and hers
and a dozen recruits. A great pearl of light
welcomed him into a tent. Inside, she was naked,
completely unveiled, his shocked and trembling reward.
For Allah is great.

WERECHIHUAHUA

He's fierce for six inches high
Is Werechihuahua.
After changing at dusk
Scampering after his prey
He often sank teeth into ankles
Hoping a victim might fall
Exposing throat to tiny teeth.
Now people don high boots
Whenever they hear the yap
Of Werechihuahua.

Small wonder he's fierce
—At least in his heart—
For the Aztecs bred him
And worshipped him
And *they* tore the hearts
Out of prisoners-of-war.

Noble families might house
A thousand Chihuahuas
Each with its own personal slave.
Imagine a thousand Chihuahuas,
Like canine piranhas reducing
Their prey to a scatter of bones
In five minutes or say half an hour.

When he retransforms at dawn
He's that funny little bootmaker

Tapping away at his bench
Coining silver from all the demand
For boots knee-high at least.

In fact not all of him
Turns into a crazed Chihuahua,
Merely the mass of his foot.
So when suspicious citizens
Peer through his window
They see that he's still abed
And never notice how the blanket
Near the end falls rather flat.

But I've spied a tiny pet dog
Burrow under the sheet
At sunrise—and why by day
Is it never about in his shop?

WINTERMUTE

Dried leaf
with stalk as rudder
scuttles like a mouse's
brown body in the breeze;

flees
the cat of the wind
which will soon shred it
leaving only the tail to drag

into a worm hole.

If people's ears
crisped to crêpe by frost
fell off and blew about in flurries
would winter be the silent season, then?

Will spring shriek anew
while fresh ears grow from nubs?
Will summer play the mad harmonica
but autumn bring us anaesthetic deafness?

That's when the worm
which hides within the brain
plugs up our hearing canals with golden wax
with roots of dead nouns, with the flaked claws

of verbs that wounded.

THREE TOKYO POEMS
FROM AROUND 1970

LOSS OF FACE

The policeman on the next corner
rubs his shave thoughtfully
as if he has picked up
—through the ether?—
my own loss of face
when I did not form squares
like the Redcoats
against this Waterloo of traffic
but scampered over the street
an illegal puppy who had to be toilet trained
in the police box,
and is adjusting his own face
just in case
I should chop him down
with my doughty samurai blade
from the toy department,
as a student in his black robot's uniform
still stabbed the bus conductor to death
the morning after
for indicating, however politely,
the No Smoking sign.

TOKYO WINTER

At first I imagined it was for
a constant supply of weak green tea
—honourable tea—
that cauldrons of water
simmered and bubbled
over the gas stoves
in every office, at every turn
—shades of the Russian stove
and the Russian samovar,
perhaps they came in with Goncharov
in the 1890s?—
however it was simply the rising steam
that interested people.
I wonder what happens in the summer
when wet is the enemy?
What subterfuge will spin-dry me
in this twelve-channel washing machine?

(The novelist Goncharov did participate significantly in a Russian naval expedition to Japan in the early 1850s to open trade negotiations through Nagasaki, at the same time as the American Admiral Perry was barging into Tokyo; but this refers to the subsequent impact of Russian novels upon Japanese authors. This reference is sheer poetic license, to be taken with many pinches of salt.)

THE WEST IS RED

The East is Red
—perhaps it's so in China
but as for here
the West is as red
on a clear winter's day
in the industrial sunset
as an opium poppy
—and people's teeth
chart the precise route of decay
in gold.
Below Tea-Water Station
they're fishing in the sewer
wearing waders and deerstalkers
but all the golden fish are already
fifty years old
swimming on the rooftops
guarded by polite young men.

POEMS & LYRICS
FROM NOVELS AND STORIES

GIORDANO BRUNO'S SONNET
'E CHI M'IMPENNA'
ADAPTED

And who will give me wings,
And who will warm my heart?
Who'll free me from the fear
Of accident and death?
Who'll snap my chains and burst the gates
Through which few people freely pass?

Aeons and years, days and hours,
The daughters and weapons of time:
Those saved me from time's fury.

That crystal sphere of the sky
Can't halt my widespread wings.
Through space I hunt infinity,
And other worlds. Once faraway,
Soon those are left behind.

(From the story "Such Dedication". Bruno, fine poet and philosopher, was imprisoned and tortured for 7 years by the Church, not to be forgiven nor forgotten, then burned alive naked in February 1600 with his tongue and palate impaled, for claiming that planets must orbit other stars, among other thoughtcrimes. "The Romantics have not his swift directness"—thus my tribute version is less than his sonnet, though at least it totals 14 lines.)

THE LOVE SONG OF JOHNNY ALIENSON: A CALYPSO

What you tell the man from the stars?
Lots of boys got Mas and Pas
Talking to them in all sorts of lingos
Aliens can't speak ours, there's the stingo!

How you love a man from the stars?
He's from a globe where girls' eyes got bars!
Girls got no bosom and their skin's hard as wood
But our boy does know how to give it to you good!

Man from the stars come to wed a woman
He'll be an ET and she'll be human
He knows his stuff but his Ma's come too
In case their wedded life needs fixing with glue

Man from the stars got himself a wife
On our own Tobago for the rest of his life
Raising his kids in an alien way
His whole damn time's a carnival day

Man from the stars he's no more than a boy
But we wish him and Marianne lots of joy
It's urgent we all get to talk to each other
So we all embrace every alien like our brother!

A Hymn of Thanksgiving

The form of Man is perfect,
It comes from God above!
And if you don't believe it,
Then you deny His love!

Our arms and legs and noses,
Our brains and breasts and bums
Are measured out in Heaven
Where God does his sums.

Satan is a shifty one,
He wants us all to change.
In labs and schools and test-tubes
He works us to derange.

The race of Man forever
Shall keep its perfect form,
So let us praise this watchword:
Adherence to the norm.

Yet we are changed, and fallen,
In an Eden without Eve.
Unlike the sinful Adam
Here we must never leave.

But when we go to Heaven
He will give us back our shapes,
For they're all still stored up there,
On God's own golden tapes.

NORMAN HARPER:
SELECTED VERSES

The embryo bird must partly die
If its wings are to emerge, to fly.
The caterpillar dies, as well,
To become the butterfly, so swell.
While man himself dies every seven
Years, but goes not up to heaven.
So here is death, and here is life:
These Siamese twins shall know no strife.
Each life is several generations
Of births and deaths like transit stations;
And then the train returns at last
To where it started, in the past.
Our death is in us, not 'out there';
It grows out of us, like our hair.
It falls like hair, like Autumn leaves;
And in the earth new life achieves.
There is no Enemy, no Thief:
A dangerous and a false belief!
Many times in life we die
So that our new mind-wings can fly;
And when we finally fold those wings,
Our spirit sings, then dies away.
There is no more; there is no Sting.
We shall be as we were before.
The day is over, perfect day.

after Friedrich Hölderlin's ***An die Parzen***
("To the Fates")

Will you let me fade in the Fall,
My kindly Powers That Be?
My poems will be ripe for plucking,
Heart's pollen will be all sweet honey
For the next year's folk.

Hullo there, Stillness, how are you?
I'm goodly glad, even if I'm not to hear
My own voice versing any more.
In my own way I've lived like Goethe.
But you know, apples overripe go rotten...

Why don't you pick my windfall, now?

(Amongst the other misrepresentations of Hölderlin's great poem, the folksy
versifier Norman Harper in my novel *Deathhunter* wilfully rendered *'Lebt' ich,
wie Götter'*—"I lived like the Gods"—as "I've lived like Goethe".)

SONG LYRICS

Get your spook on, John
Get your demon screamin'
There's hell in your head
And you're seein' red
    It's nanoware time tonight

There's a ghoul in your brain
And you're goin' insane
Your power's a-risin'
Over hell's horizon
    It's nanoware time tonight
    It's nanoware time tonight
    It's nanoware time tonight

MANA POEMS

POEM
(BY EYENO NURMI)

I bathed in a spring, imagining
A bird with tripe on its beak,
Squawking: "The snake and its servant
Are two, and one besides."
Oh black men of Pootara,
Why can't you hark to cuckoos?

Two cuckoos sat in a curver tree
And cackled, *Ukoo*, at the sky
Where the silver sickle unpeeled
A potato moon on high.
Oh black men of Pootara,
Why can't you hark to cuckoos?

A gossip sat in a harper tree,
With a wax bloom in its beak.
Oh where is the Queen's bed of love?
That's the very place I seek.
Oh black men of Pootara,
Why can't you hark to cuckoos?

Cuckoo's mate perched in a minty tree
Soon to explode into flames.
Blossom forth, undeflowered,
Unlock the volcano of names!
Oh black men of Pootara,
Why can't you hark to cuckoos?

***

She who would steer me seeks
The name of the bloom
A gingerbread woman wears
In her ginger hairs.
Her words shall melt like candlewax,
Reform to shape that name.
Oh black men of Pootara,
Why can't you hark to cuckoos
When a town is melted by candle-fire?

A RIDDLE
(BY EYENO NURMI)

What is my name but a bloom's?
What is my name but a flower's?
For chimneyflowers are my lady's fingers,
Long and azure and far-reaching;
Ringing with stories, far-hearing;
Pink heartbells are her toenails,
And her fingernails: yellow narciss;
What is her navel but a milkcup?
What starflowers spark in her eyes?
What am I then but a bright daisy?
Alas we guessed wrong; three tries!

What am I then but the bloom
Unfurling its bloody petals
Through a bed of virgin snow,
Piercing the soft frigid wool
In violation of its whiteness,
Deflowering by its flowering,
Fragrance of rape and murder.

But no, I'm not the bloodflower,
So guess again, guess thrice!
What flower seems of candlewax,
Creamy petals curly as ears?
I bloom in moon-child meadows;
I can outlive the years—

Fitting

A key
Slides into emptiness
Of the same shape as itself
And turns that emptiness around.

A Lament

Not missing my supper,
No, missing my sister,
Missing her yellow silk hair,
Missing Eyeno reciting,
Her blue eye inviting
Not a kiss but a prayer
From her brother: *forgiving*
For the thorn in the heart
The prick in the loins
Virgin yet violating.
Moon lying under a lake
Being no reflection, ah no,
Being no moon in our sky.
In a moon departing,
In a moon, a stone moon!
Ukko, Ukko: *why?*

Gelding me, sickle in the sky,
Trimming my words to make
amends,
Shaving me, shriving me—

Ukko, Ukko: *why?*

BALLADS, SONGS
AND TANGO

The Tale of Jordi

Did the saint slay the dragon?
Did the saint save the girl?
Did the girl cheer the saint?
    Oh no, roll over!

While the dragon lay a-dying
Did the girl kiss her hero?
Did the hero kiss the girl?
    Oh no, roll over!

No, the girl loved her dragon
So she spat at the saint
So the saint slew the girl,
    Oh yes, roll over!

Did the snake love the girl?
Did he wind round her waist?
Bruise her breathless breasts?
    Oh yes, roll over!

Did the snake lick her loins
With the fork of a tongue?
Did his head slide inside?
    Oh yes, roll over!

Was his body as smooth
And as slippery as silk?
Did he flex and twist?
    Oh yes, roll over!

Was he firm as could be?
Did his tail grip her knee?
Did she moisten his neck?
 Oh yes, roll over!

Did the snake shed his skin
Owing to her juices within
Thus shutting her wombdoor,
 Jatta?

Did the maid touch her knife?
Did she bare her breast?
Did she prick her skin?
 Or else roll over?

Did her red blood flow
All down to her toe?
Did her dark hair cascade?
 Was Jatta afraid?

Did her heart beat fast?
Was a lover forecast?
In the space of a dream,
 Oh yes, roll over!

Will she come the next day?
Come grey, or sun's ray?
So what will her dragon say?
 But: roll over!

Did Jatta shed her clothes?
Did she romp in the lough?
Did the gold splash her skin?
 Oh yes, roll over!

Did the girl turn her back?
Whatever did she lack
But a thumb in the crack?
 Oh yes, roll over!

Excerpt From a Variation on The Tale of Jordi

He saved her from a snake,
He did it for her sake
But it was all a mistake;
She loved the snake, not him.

The Tangomeister's Song

Why don't we part
Before we start
To fall in love with one another?
Why not save ourselves the bother
Of two broken hearts?
An Ukko's in the sky tonight, dear
heart;
A cuckoo's keeping its eye on us two
lovers.

Now I'm as far away from you as any
Ukko,
And the cuckoo is our only voice,
Mocking me that you still love me,
Cheating you that I have made
Another choice, another choice.

Why did you send me so far away
To a land beyond the seas?
You loved another, but now every day
I shall trouble your heart with unease.

Sky-sickle shines upon the sea
Silver combs in your hair
You're as far away from me
Without a care, without a care...

Another Tangomeister's Song

This is a night as never will be.
You'll go back to sea and never see me,
Not again, oh my dusky mariner.

Cast a sway on me
And never set me free
Till the stars drown in the sea.

CHILDREN'S SONG

Oh our home is here,
      So what do we care
If our home was elsewhere
      Once?

Well here we are now,
      Clasp hands and chant,
And banish the memory of
      Once!

Put Once in a pail
      With a handful of hail
And throw it in yon
      Pond!

THE MUTANT'S SONG

My body's a beast's, not a man's,
Yet my heart's as human as yours.
Dear girl, my duckling, I beg of you
Don't close, don't lock your doors.
The voice of sorrow is silence,
And the name of absence is, ah my lost Rita.
I'd chance almost any violence
From her false lover just to seat her
      By my side
      By my lonely side.

There's a girl who's going away
On the very next day, the very next day
For ever, and a Sunday.

There's a girl who's broken my heart,
And tomorrow morn my hen will depart.
In the arms of an upstart she'll play.

Tomorrow night she'll bare her breasts
In a goose-feather bed she'll be caressed—

THE MUTANT'S SECOND SONG

To you I may look like a beast,
To your eyes I may seem nature's jest.
One pitying glance from you, Rita, the least
Little nod, and love beats a drum in my
breast.

You're such a fine hen, charming chick,
Dainty bird—any man will avow.
How it wounds me to the quick
When a *beast* can't woo a *bird*, thou.

Dear duckling, you'll forever be my only.
Yet ne'er I'll tiptoe to your downy nest.
Forever must my aching heart be lonely,
Never shall my love for you be blessed.

THE MUTANT'S THIRD SONG

We're so different, yet the same
At heart: a mocky-girl, and prince.
Why ever should I be to blame
For yielding to your hints?

A princess and a mocky-man;
He came to her palace door.
Her brother had ravished his sister
Whom he had claimed to adore.

The Mutant's Fourth Song

Within, I'm the same as any other,
Can't you, won't you, call me
brother?
I lost my love beyond the blue sea,
Beyond the blue sky, beyond the
blue stars.
She alone ever once kissed me
On my strange blue skin,
On my deep blue skin, so pitifully.

THE MUTANT'S FIFTH SONG

Losing your voice from my mind, my Lord,
Your dear tones slipping away,
Leaving me alone without a word
Ever again to be saying

Unless to a child, a sister, a lover
Instead of yourself, my Lord gone missing.
How much perfection am I putting aside
In exchange for the hugging and kissing?

The Mutant's Sixth Song

Oh where's my lass who lacks an eye?
She turned away, she cannot spy
Me searching desperately.
She thinks I'm playing blind
But it's *me* she left behind.

Oh where's my lass who lacks an ear?
I'm calling but she cannot hear
Me crying crazily.
She thinks I'm playing dumb
Though my heart beats like a drum.

Oh where's my love who lacks a mouth?
Did she go north, or was it south—?

THE MUTANT'S SEVENTH SONG

How can I kiss the lips in my mind
When those same lips swallow me?
How can I set out, a love to find,
When there is no hollow in me?

FROM
THE BOOK OF THE
LAND OF HEROES

Thus the smith awhile lived wifeless,
And without his wife grew older.
Then a maid rose from the furnace,
And her figure all was lovely.
Others greatly shuddered at her,
But the smith he was not frightened.
After that he laid the maiden
On the softest of the blankets,
Smoothed for her the softest pillows.
On the silken bed he laid her.
At the maiden's side he stretched him...

***

As a lad, young Tycho Cammon,
Son of Ivan, and his lady
Sophie of the family Donner,
She who hailed from Verin Meadow,
Also known as Verinitty,
Named because attacks by wild beasts
In the past had posed a problem
Till the Donners in their wisdom
Fenced their fields with words and palings
To exclude the savage raiders
Then set poison bait near beast-dens
Brewed from fungi by a shaman
Known as Edvin son of Hubert
Who had come from Kippan country...

(AS CHANTED BY THE GIRLEM)

Maids of Horror, Menace Lasses,
Sent the fly that bit his earlobe,
Putting poison in his bloodstream,
Baneful toxin, blighting venom,
Gnawing at the Prince's kidneys,
Causing lesions and pink urine,
Robbing him of mana-power,
Gagging all his proclamations;
Jinx and Jinxie, Minx and Minxie
Are the names of those four pixies,
Daughters of a fatal wedding
Of a mutant and the fastboy,
Son of Jatta who sought safety
In the hall of Lord van Maanen.

The name of the fly was *Minxie*,
Begetter of his malady,
Milady of his misfortune,
Be purged from his healing waters,
That words from his heart speak strongly,
And a man with two minds may know
Fragrance of flowers, zest of food,
For *love* is the name of release!

***

Show me, star-cairn, guide my charcoal,
Picture me the path to elsewhere;

135

Let me find the source of mana,
Heart of Ukko hidden from us,
Shining forth upon disciple,
Hurling Arvid from his saddle...

***

Simpering daughter, dancing, kissing,
Father finding daughter missing,
Comes the rascal from the tower,
Thinking only to deflower.

Flash of emerald and sapphire,
Eager fingers would acquire,
Fingers black and bodies velvet,
Pompous serpents send their pets.

L<small>AST</small> R<small>ITES</small> <small>FOR</small> S<small>OLDIERS</small>
(CHANTED BY A MANA-PRIEST)

The swan flies—

Who will gather the feathers it drops?
Who will gather your bones from a distant forest?
Still left on the shelf is your harmonica;
Still here on the wall is your fishing net.
Like white sylvester trees or ivorywood
The grieving girls are left.

In spring when cuckoos cackle of lust
Where will you be then, my boy,
Apple of our eye? And on sauna night
What hens will hope for delight?
For the last time mother beats you
And the beasts are in sister's care.

Mother, oh mother, why cry?
Your son's toys stay behind!
I lay you in a coffin;
I bury you in a grave.
Don't cut off your toe to lame yourself
Or your lord will shave your head.

CONJURATION

Lady, coming to my bower,
Take from me these words of power:
Thrust at lust, and cage my rage,
Be the mistress of my plagues.
Lucky hour, or evil hour?
Man, or mage? War to wage?
Blank stays your page
If your soul is sage.
Deflower and devour:
Oh I empower adjustment.
Be eloquent
      magniloquent
          malevolent
              turbulent
                  virulent
take from me these words of power
lady coming while I flower...

COLLABORATIONS WITH
MIKE ALLEN

INVERTED UNIVERSE

When the universe inverts, we will breathe
earth as if it were air, fly below limestone
and granite toward the soothing coolness
of the magma core, on hands and knees
scale the worm-infested underside of the ocean.

The sun will be dark but all shadows bright
in a zebra landscape, and the moon in its phases
will wax with blackness, wane with light
against a luminous night sky patterned
by the black dots of the inky way.

Our next lunar expedition will no longer
be a matter of rocket science. We'll mine
our way to the moon, carve a tunnel through
the white gulfs of space, begin our cold
lives anew inside Luna's amniotic warmth.

When the universe inverts, we'll have silly dreams
as we perform our daily tasks like zombies
while in our sleep you and I will meet and make love
with such full awareness and in perfect secrecy
being alone together at last, but not until then.

We'll struggle, in our passions, with the shapes
of inverted sex, explore the textures inside
each other's skin; you in your bed, me in mine,
hearts calm with ecstasy, united by warm soil
and rock that carry the waves of our desire.

KATAGENESIS

A reverse synthetic transformation
is the conversion of plastic back into oil
willed by goddess Gaea, so that credit cards
stain our dissolving shirts, glass falls from windows,
melting carrier bags dump blackening milk.

Beautiful women bleed prehistoric blood,
their plastic surgeries undone; politicians
ooze tar from plastic smiles; puddles 'R' Disneyland,
and I and you and we all liquefy—
our fake lives stain the ground like so much crude.

Propitiating Cthulhu

When the ancient alien one slid towards me
phosphorescent slime exerting eldritch mesmerism
huge miscegenation of sea-anemone and squid
mostly indescribable by any human words
my knees jellified so down I knelt before it.
In this dire predicament appeared only one way
to propitiate such monstrosity—namely

by Cthulhulingus. The elder thing halted,
aquiver with androgynous cosmic lust
which transmuted my tongue and lips
to monstrous proportions. After an hour
of oral worship I slumped to the cavern floor
forever deformed but grateful to be alive.

As the Old One departed, pseudopod fibres
propelled from my sinuses of their own
curling accord, wriggling away as worms.
They now enter sleeping men's and women's ears
at night, tormenting them with disgusting desires
born from my swallowed shame. Forgive me!
I alone have snarfed Cthulhu's pubic hair.

SEVENTH COMING

After the heathens martyred Jesus 6.6,
demolished Him in a crowded, crazed arena,
cornered, bound, chainsawed, crushed,
the ethereal execs in the celestial penthouse
vowed to make the next model indestructible.

So many attempts at pacifying this planet!
The many Messiahs inserted into Palestine
to begin with, perfectly mimicking human form,
'taking on flesh,' as the saying went; one Messiah
in particular became rather famous.

And what sprang from Him? Crusaders,
massacres, pogroms, bonfires, a church *militant*.
Buddha, alias Jesus 5.7, was a better model,
J-E-S-U-S in the sing-song of the butterfly aliens
signifying the taming of aggressive savages

but the brutes' penchant for bloodlust ran
so deep, those who heeded one model would
kill the next one's followers (and the model
Himself, if they got their hands on Him.)
The board met in their luxurious pocket universe

to discuss the design of Jesus 7.0; for the first
time in eons, hawk factions outvoted the doves.
Let weapons break against His undamaged flesh,
they said; let Him sway the masses, not through
argument, but through telepathic mind control.

Some among them fluttered energy-wings
in coloured blurs of butterfly distress; but most
rolled up tongues into tight knots of determination.
By then the savages had trashed their civilisation,
if worthy of the word, when other words for it

were Auschwitz and Hiroshima, Rwanda, Pol Pot
and Twin Towers, virus plague and nerve gas.
The Earth was on her beam ends, on the skids,
balkanised and chaotic, though black laboratories
still beavered away at offense and defense.

Protected by force field, Jesus 7.0 arrived, radiated
commands to be meek, mild, and butterfly-friendly.
Having watched the old movies and read the old books
the savages knew how to respond to alien invasion.
Ramp up! Unite! Devise telepathy blockers and devices

to analyse and penetrate a force field and tease
its secrets, and many others, from Jesus 7.0.
This time no crucifixion or bloodcurdling doom
for Him; instead, reverse engineering.
Yeah verily, at last, He had brought Salvation.

SEVENTY TIMES SEVEN

is four-hundred and ninety, the number of times
he committed adultery during twenty years of marriage.
His compulsion, his itch women chose not to resist,
the very speed of the conquests ensuring their safety,
for he would move on compulsively before any bond

could form and before any heart could be broken.
They simply savoured his perfected methods (who wouldn't?)
but she always knew (and he knew that she knew)
for she sensed scents; yet since she was a Christian
and already longsuffering, she forgave from the first.

Soon he would even tell her, not quite like Scheherazade,
of ventures to the Oriental market, the wilds of Africa,
the exotic shores (and shades) of Caucasian nationalities,
of exploring the realms of the obese and undernourished,
of lessons given to the young and learned from the old.

She took strange pleasure in the saga of his infidelities,
always numbering them in diaries and in her mind,
giving thanks that he saw her as his anchor, his pole star,
his axis and pivot and centre of gravity. Religiously
she counted till the twentieth year, when he made love

to number four ninety-one; and when he came home
she put him to sleep with an anaesthetic dart
and when he came round he found she had crucified him
in the cellar of their home; a poster of a haloed Jesus
hung opposite. At first he tried to reason with her

that the advice to forgive exactly seventy times seven times
applied to Peter's brother, not his wife. Soon his lips,
which had kissed so many mouths, were parched
but she provided cool water through a straw
either mercifully or to prolong his ordeal.

On the third day of his passion, despite pain and exhaustion,
he rose compulsively and she worshipped him.

TimeFlood

Why did they dam the river of time some way upstream?
How did they dam time itself? Maybe they fought—*will fight*—
a probability war, striving to block some streams of possibility
and reinforce others. A myriad dams might be made. Sabotage
may ensue, and rival dams, to divert events a different way.

The result is that time flooded backward catastrophically,
causing such eddies and whirlpools and deeps and shallows.
A billion people lived their whole lives in mere seconds
and expired in ignorance. Others were flotsam on the flood,
seeing cities and civilisations rise and fall around them.

Caught up in an eddy, a mother-to-be found herself
kneeling at the grave of her great-granddaughter. Stretched
by the current, a soldier shot dead in a two-second war
suckled for centuries at his mother's tit. By the time he hit
the ground a glacier was engulfing the battlefield.

And me? And me? She grew instantly old
in my shrinking arms as I became a child again,
held tight by a blind crone. I lead her along
by her wrinkled hand, my grandmother so it seems,
who still whispers endearments toothlessly

As we make our way though the ruins of millennia,
wrecked rude huts, tumbled temples of marble,
fallen castles, twisted girders of skyscrapers,
and so much mud where at least food grows,
in search of an Eden from where time may have sprung,

A fountain of youth to restore to her some
of my unwanted juvenility. But this Earth
of multiple eras is vast, survivors are few
and mostly insane, and yesterday for the first time
I saw, to my horror, the corpse of a dinosaur.

Zombie Bombs

Now they fall in clusters,
sticky masses of squirming black
titanic insects' egg sacs
that plummet past the towers,
splatter in the streets to spew
cores of moving dead.
Those not shredded on impact
crawl from the red pulp,
often too broken to stand,
lifting their softened heads
to quest for us in some way
we cannot understand.

At first they fell in ones and twos, these sacs,
and emergency services
could cope, medics striving to
assist just as at a plane crash.
But soon volunteers were shovelling
squirming protoplasm into trucks.
Some helpers were engulfed, suffocated.
The rain of living dead
increased, burst and broken, unable
to die. The army brought flame-throwers.
Did the steam scream?

No sonic booms announced
the bombings. I remember

the first time I saw a ship,
a dark movement in the sky
like a whale's lumpy back breaking
an ocean surface turned upside down;
then gone. Moments later bodies burst,
limbs writhed on lawns, roofs, driveways.
When mobile flesh began to push
against my front door, I nailed
towels in place. On TV soon:
skyfalls in Japan, India, Brazil...

Will we invent matter transmitters
and fill interspace with echo-copies
which enraged aliens cleanse thus?
Will aliens decide to genocide us—
doubly, by dumping upon the past?
Is this merely the garbage collection
of overpopulation from future Earth-hive?

If many realities exist, ours is chosen
as a necro-dump, while brighter timelines
sail onward blithely. Or may this be
the Second Coming of everyone who ever lived,
a Devilish miracle? For God has died
and now an even greater blackness
bloats the sky. The living dead are voiceless.

How desperately I wished they would speak,
my own throat closed in breathless fear
at what they might say—or what story
I might tell. For by ghastly "luck"
while watching the latest horrors
from Mexico, a news camera zoomed close
and I saw my own fouled gasping face:

same brown eyes, same eyebrow scar,
beard greyer, thinner. My hand groped

toward the newsman; on my ring finger
I recognized my widower's band.
I can't get to Mexico in time
to stop myself from being burned,
bulldozed, buried. If I could,
if I stared into my own ruined face,
could I unstop my throat to scream:
How and when will I fall from the sky?

INDEX OF FIRST LINES

M

A mighty computer rules France 54
Maids of Horror, Menace Lasses 135
Memories rewrite themselves; photos remind us 25
Mister Stone, Mister Stone, when you die 32
My body's a beast's, not a man's 127
My fingers make 28

N

Not missing my supper 117
Now they fall in clusters 150

O

Oh our home is here 126
Oh where's my lass who lacks an eye 132

P

The policeman on the next corner 99
Probably there'd be some innocent victims 93

R

A reverse synthetic transformation 142

S

The swan flies 137

T

This is a night as never will be 125
Three-legged pooch runs down the street 80
Thus the smith awhile lived wifeless 134
To you I may look like a beast 128

W

We're so different, yet the same 129
We tried to help daughter Amanda 27

ACKNOWLEDGMENTS

"Abductee" *star*line* 2001

"Andromeda" *Whores of Babylon* 1988

"Catalogue Note by the Artist" *Asimov's Science Fiction* 2013

"Cobwebs in Heaven" *Mythic Delirium* 2006

"Counterfactual Photos" *Mythic Delirium* 2011

"Death by Dyslexia" *Mythic Delirium* 2000

"Entertaining a Hope" *Mythic Delirium* 2003

"Exprisonment" *Star*Line* 2003

"Fones" *Weird Tales* 2004

"Fossil Man" *Dreams and Nightmares* 1999

"Ghetto Blaster" *Star*Line* 2001

"Giordano Bruno's sonnet 'E chi m'impenna' adapted" *Interzone* 1996

"Good Heavens, Mr Evans" *Dreams and Nightmares* 1999

"A Hymn of Thanksgiving" *Converts* 1984

"In Praise of Spam" *Star*Line* 2004

"Inverted Universe" (with Mike Allen) *Star*Line* 2002

"Katagenesis" (with Mike Allen) *Tales of the Talisman* 2008

"Let There Be Darkness: an Origin Myth" *The Lexicographer's Love Song and Other Poems* 2001

"The Lexicographer's Love Song" *Weird Tales* 2001

"The Love Song of Johnny Alienson: A Calypso" *The Book of Ian Watson* 1985

"Marsupials in our Midst: the Explorer of Mirabella Rehearses his Tale" *Altair* 1999

"Memory Man" *Asimov's Science Fiction* 2003

"Never Ever" *Dreams and Nightmares* 2001

"The Next French Revolution" *The Lexicographer's Love Song and Other Poems* 2001

"Norman Harper: Selected Verses" *Deathhunter* 1981

"Oh Happy Franz!" *The Lexicographer's Love Song and Other Poems* 2001

"Otherwhys" *Weird Tales* 1998
"Owed to my Screen Saver" *Weird Tales* 1999
"The Pleasure Surgeons" *Dreams and Nightmares* 2002
"Propitiating Cthulhu" (with Mike Allen) *Illumen* 2004
"The Quantum Stalker Woos Miss Jones" *Dreams and Nightmares* 2000
"Root Canal Therapy" *Back Brain Recluse* 1989
"Screams" *Asimov's Science Fiction* 2008
"Seventh Coming" (with Mike Allen) *Strange Horizons* 2002
"Seventy times seven" (with Mike Allen) *Albedo One* 2003
"Smoke" *Fantasycon 2009 Souvenir Programme* 2009
"Song Lyrics" *Asimov's Science Fiction* 1989
"A Sort of Hysteresis" *Mythic Delirium* 2003
"Surgeons of the Soul" *Mythic Delirium* 2001
"Three-legged Dog" *Interzone* 1999
"Three Tokyo Poems from around 1970"
          ("Loss of Face", "Tokyo Winter", and
          "The West is Red") *Cidereal Times* 1979
"The Time Traveller Instructs and Implores" *Star★Line* 1999
"TimeFlood" (with Mike Allen) *Asimov's Science Fiction* 2005
"To His Coy, or Greedy, Bimbo" *Recombination Progress Report 2* 2007
"True Love" *Weird Tales* 2001
"Universe Zoo" *Star★Line* 2000
"Unreal Messages?" *Asimov's Science Fiction* 2001
"The Virgin and the Suicide Bomber" *Puny Earthling* 2006
"Werechihuahua" *Mythic Delirium* 2002
"Wintermute" *Tand* 1990
"Zombie Bombs" (with Mike Allen) *Helix: Speculative Fiction Quarterly* 2008

Ballads, Songs, Riddles, Chants, Conjurations, Laments, and Tangos are
original to *Lucky's Harvest* (1993) and *The Fallen Moon* (1994), apart from
"Another Tangomeister's Song" which appeared in the associated story 'The
Shortest Night', *Asimov's Science Fiction* 1998.

www.ingramcontent.com/pod-product-compliance
Lightning Source LLC
Chambersburg PA
CBHW030129260626
47156CB00008B/2859